Mr. Maurer

Karen's Grandad

Look for these
and other books about Karen
in the
Baby-sitters Little Sister series:

Little Sister

Karen's Grandad
Ann M. Martin

Illustrations by Susan Tang

A
LITTLE APPLE
PAPERBACK

SCHOLASTIC INC.
New York Toronto London Auckland Sydney

ISBN 0-590-26280-7

12 11 10 9 8 7 6 5 4 3 2 1   6 7 8 9/9 0 1/0

Printed in the U.S.A.   40

First Scholastic printing, February 1996

The author gratefully acknowledges
Stephanie Calmenson
for her help
with this book.

Karen's Grandad

1

Switching Houses

I woke up on Thursday morning feeling very cozy. I was in my warm bed, wearing my pink flannel pajamas. But it was time to get up. I could not stay in bed one more minute.

"Today is an important day," I said to Moosie, my stuffed cat.

It was the first day of February. I was waking up at my big house. I had been living at the big house for two months. I would be going to sleep at my little house. I would live there for one month. I will tell

you later why I have two houses. But first I will tell you who I am.

My name is Karen Brewer. I am seven years old. I have blonde hair, blue eyes, and a bunch of freckles. I wear glasses. I have two pairs. I wear my blue pair for reading. I wear my pink pair the rest of the time. When I switch houses I have to be very sure I do not forget either pair.

Switching houses is the reason I had to get up right away. I had a lot of good-byes to say. I also had to pack a few things to take to the little house with me.

So why was I still in bed? Because it was warm and cozy.

"Okay, Moosie. I am going to count down from three. Then I will get up," I said. "Three . . . two . . . one . . . up!"

I jumped out of bed and got dressed. I put on the red sweater and matching socks Mommy had given me for Christmas. I put on navy blue leggings. Then I hurried downstairs for breakfast. My whole big-house family was there.

Andrew was there, too. Andrew is my little brother. He is four going on five. Andrew and I switch houses together.

Andrew looked the way I felt. Kind of sad. I always feel a little sad when I leave one house to go to the other. I have been through this lots of times. So I knew just how it worked.

Before I left for school, I said good-bye to everyone. The people who live at the big house are Daddy, Elizabeth, Nannie, Kristy, David Michael, Emily Michelle, Sam, and Charlie. (I will tell you more about them later.) This is how I did it.

When I finished breakfast, I hugged each person. When my jacket was on and I was walking out the door, I waved. When I was walking down the street to the school bus stop, I called, "Good-bye, everyone! I will be back in a month. Good-bye!"

The next thing I did was say hi to Hannie. Hannie Papadakis is one of my two best friends. She was waiting at the bus stop when I got there.

4

"Hi, Karen. I just remembered you are switching houses today. I will miss riding to school with you," said Hannie.

"I will miss that, too," I replied.

There it was again. Being sad and being happy. I was sad I would not be riding the big-house school bus with Hannie. But I would be happy when I rode the little-house school bus with Nancy. (Nancy Dawes is my other best friend.)

I was also going to be gigundoly happy when I saw my granny and grandad. They usually live in Nebraska. But they had been staying at the little house since November. It was kind of a winter vacation.

We had almost reached school. The sad part of my day was over. All that was left was the happy part. After school, I was going to the little house. Hooray!

2

An Excellent Two-Two

The reason I live in two houses is not so unusual. It is because my parents are divorced.

A long time ago, when I was little, I lived in one big house in Stoneybrook, Connecticut, with Mommy, Daddy, and Andrew. Then Mommy and Daddy started fighting a lot. I did not like that at all. After a while, they told Andrew and me that they love us very much, but they could not get along with each other anymore. So they decided to get divorced.

6

After the divorce, Mommy moved with Andrew and me to the little house, which is not far away from the big house. Then she met a very nice man named Seth. Mommy and Seth got married. That is how Seth became my stepfather. So now Mommy, Seth, Andrew, and I live at the little house with Midgie (Seth's dog) and Rocky (Seth's cat), Emily Junior (my pet rat), and Bob (Andrew's hermit crab). And I told you that Granny and Grandad have been living with us since November. Their real home is in Nebraska.

After the divorce, Daddy stayed at the big house. (It is the house he grew up in.) Then he met Elizabeth. Daddy and Elizabeth got married. That is how Elizabeth became my stepmother.

Elizabeth was married once before and has four children. You already know their names. But you do not know how old they are. David Michael is seven; Kristy is thirteen; Sam and Charlie are so old they are in high school.

Daddy and Elizabeth adopted Emily Michelle from a faraway country called Vietnam. Emily is two and a half. She is lots of fun and I love her a lot. That is why I named my pet rat after her.

Nannie is Elizabeth's mother. That makes her my stepgrandmother. She came to help take care of Emily. But she really helps take care of everyone.

Let me see. Who did I leave out? Oh, yes. The pets. They are Shannon, David Michael's big Bernese mountain dog puppy; Boo-Boo, Daddy's cranky old cat; Crystal Light the Second, my goldfish; and Gold-fishie, Andrew's pony. (Just kidding. You know what Goldfishie is. Don't you?)

I have a special name for Andrew and me. I call us Andrew Two-Two and Karen Two-Two. That is because we have two of so many things. (I thought of those names after my teacher read a book to our class. It was called *Jacob Two-Two Meets the Hooded Fang*.) Andrew and I have two mommies and two daddies, two houses and two fam-

8

ilies, two cats and two dogs. I have two of lots of other things. I have two bicycles, one at each house. Andrew has two tricycles. I have two stuffed cats. Moosie lives at the big house. Goosie lives at the little house. I have two pieces of Tickly, my special blanket.

Having two of so many things makes going back and forth a lot easier.

I even have my two best friends. Nancy lives next door to the little house. Hannie lives across the street and one house over from the big house. Nancy and Hannie and I are in the same second-grade class at Stoneybrook Academy. (We call ourselves the Three Musketeers.)

Andrew and I switch houses almost every month. Sometimes we stay at one house or the other for two months. Either way works out fine for me. I have many talents in life. And one of my talents is being an excellent two-two.

3

How Are You Feeling Today?

By Monday I was settled into the little house. I rode the bus to school with Nancy.

"Please be seated, everyone," said Ms. Colman when we arrived. "Natalie, would you take attendance this morning?"

Oh, boy. I decided I had better get comfortable. Natalie is the slowest attendance taker in class. She worries about making mistakes. I looked over her shoulder to make sure she was doing things right.

First she checked off her own name. Then she checked off my name and Ricky

Torres's name. (Ricky is my pretend husband. We got married on the playground at recess one day.) The three of us sit at the front of the classroom together. That is because we wear glasses and Ms. Colman says we can see better up front.

Next Natalie checked off Pamela Harding, Jannie Gilbert, and Leslie Morris. (They are best friends, kind of like the Three Musketeers. Pamela also happens to be my best enemy.)

These are the other kids Natalie checked off: Addie Sidney, who rolled into class late in her wheelchair (her bus was having trouble that week); Bobby Gianelli, who lives near the little house and used to be a bully, but is now mostly my friend; Terri and Tammy Barkan, who are twins; Audrey Green; Hank Reubens; Ian Johnson; Omar Harris; Chris Lamar; Hannie, and Nancy.

Sara Ford was out sick.

Natalie checked over the list one more time. Then she handed the book to Ms. Colman. Whew!

"Thank you, Natalie," said Ms. Colman. "I have an announcement to make, class."

Hmm. I like Ms. Colman's Surprising Announcements best. Her most surprising announcement came last month. She told us that she is going to have a baby. We gave her a baby shower and everything. I could tell this was just a regular announcement, though. I wondered what it would be.

"Before I make my announcement, I want to ask you a question," said Ms. Colman. "How are you feeling today?"

Huh? I wondered why Ms. Colman was asking. She called on a few kids.

"Bobby, how are you today?" asked Ms. Colman.

"Okay, I guess. Only I feel a little cranky because my sister, Alicia, was up sick last night," replied Bobby.

"Karen, how are you feeling?" asked Ms. Colman.

"I am feeling happy because my granny and grandad are still living at my house."

Ms. Colman asked a few more kids her

12

question. Then she made her announcement, "We are going to begin a new unit
today," she said. "You have helped me
start it. The unit is about feelings. And you
have each just told me how you feel. Bobby
feels cranky. Karen feels happy. Can you
name some other feelings?"

Pamela raised her hand. She said that
anger is a feeling. Nancy said sadness is a
feeling. After that, no one could think of
any others.

Ms. Colman helped us out.

"What if there is going to be a party. How
do you feel?" she asked.

"Excited!" we replied.

"What if no one comes to your party.
How do you feel?" asked Ms. Colman.

"Disappointed!" we replied. We were
catching on.

Then Ms. Colman gave us a homework
assignment to start us on our new unit
about feelings.

"I would like each of you to bring in a
book about a feeling or feelings," said Ms.

Colman. "It can be a chapter book or a picture book. We will share our books and our feelings about them."

Do you want to know how I felt about that assignment? I will tell you. I felt very good because I love books.

Talking to Grandad

When I got home from school, Mommy and Granny were in the kitchen unpacking groceries. Grandad was resting in bed. (Granny's and Grandad's bed was a fold-out couch in the den. We had turned the den into a very nice bedroom for them.)

"Hi, Grandad," I said. "Want some company?"

"You know I always love your company, Karen," Grandad replied.

"I am going to ask Mommy if I can have

my after-school snack in here. Do you want a snack, too?"

"No, thank you," replied Grandad. "I am not too hungry these days."

I washed up while Mommy made me a snack of peanut butter on crackers, and apple juice. She said I could bring it to Grandad's room.

Grandad was resting with his eyes closed. I looked around while I ate my snack. The room was small. That was too bad because Grandad was used to living in a big, open farmhouse. And he was used to working outside in his garden. It was one of his favorite things. Being in a little room could not be so cheerful for him. It was a gray, gloomy day, too. Just then Grandad opened his eyes and smiled at me.

"You are back," he said. "How was school today? I would like to hear all about it."

"Well, first of all, Natalie got to take attendance instead of me because it was her turn. She is so slow," I said. "And Ms.

Colman started a new unit about feelings. Our homework assignment is to bring in a book that is about a feeling or feelings."

"That sounds like a very good unit," said Grandad. "It is important to understand your feelings. It is easier to live with feelings when you make friends with them. Even the difficult ones. Now, what book are you thinking about bringing in?"

"I have not decided yet," I replied. "I like *The Rabbits' Wedding* a lot."

"We read that book together," said Grandad. "But I am not sure I can remember the story. Will you tell me what it is about?"

I have read the book a lot of times and know it very well. I reminded Grandad of the story.

"It is about a little black rabbit and a little white rabbit, who play in a forest together," I said. "They play Hop Skip And Jump Me, and Hide And Seek. They play Jump The Daisies, and Run Through The Clover. They have fun and are happy. Only sometimes the little black rabbit gets sad. He

17

wishes he could be with the little white rabbit forever and ever. Do you remember the rest, Grandad?"

"I would like you to tell it to me," Grandad replied.

"Well, the little white rabbit tells the little black rabbit to wish very, very hard for them to be together always. They tuck dandelions behind their ears. Then the other animals in the forest come and dance a wedding dance around them because the rabbits are happy and in love," I said.

"Ah, yes. I remember it now. It is about feeling happy, sad, and in love," said Grandad. "What about *Alexander and the Terrible, Horrible, No Good, Very Bad Day*? You used to like that book."

"That book is funny," I said. "Everything keeps going wrong for Alexander one day. He feels so grumpy. He keeps saying he is going to move to Australia. But his mom says things can go wrong in Australia, too."

We talked about books we like.

"Why don't you bring some books in

18

here? We can read them together," said Grandad.

"Okay! I will be right back," I replied.

I came back with just one book. I knew it was the one I wanted to share. It was *The Velveteen Rabbit*.

Good Books

The next day at school, Ms. Colman said, "I am looking forward to hearing about the books you brought in. Please tell the class about the feelings in your books. Who would like to begin?"

My hand shot up before anyone else's. So Ms. Colman called on me first.

"I brought in *The Velveteen Rabbit*," I said. "It is about love. A toy rabbit becomes real because a little boy loves him."

"That is one of my favorite stories," said Ms. Colman, smiling. "How does the boy

20

show that he loves the rabbit?"

"The boy talks with him and plays with him. He hugs him and kisses him. He will not even go to sleep without the rabbit at his side," I replied. "At the end of the book, a fairy turns the toy into a real breathing, hopping rabbit. She says only toys who have been truly loved can come alive that way."

"Thank you very much for sharing that book, Karen," said Ms. Colman. "Who else would like to share a book?"

Bobby raised his hand.

"The book I brought in is called *My Grandson Lew*," said Bobby. "It is about a boy named Lew who misses his grandfather. His grandfather used to baby-sit for Lew when Lew was really little. Then his grandfather died."

"How did Lew feel?" asked Ms. Colman.

"He felt sad. He wanted to see his grandfather again. But he knew he never would," said Bobby. "So Lew and his mother remember things about Lew's grandfather together. That makes them both feel better."

Poor Lew. I was lucky. My grandad was at home in my very own house.

Ms. Colman called on Ricky next.

"My book is *Everett Anderson's Goodbye*," said Ricky. "Everett Anderson is a boy whose daddy died. He has lots of different feelings. First he cannot believe it. Then he is angry. Then he makes believe he can bring his daddy back if he is very good all the time. But he cannot bring him back so he gets really sad. Then time passes and he starts to feel better. He knows that even if his daddy is not around, his daddy's love still is."

Wow. That was a very good book report. I was gigundoly proud of my pretend husband, Ricky.

Ms. Colman walked to Ricky's desk.

"This book is another favorite of mine," she said.

She picked up Ricky's book and read to us from the end of it: *"Whatever happens*

when people die, love doesn't stop, and neither will I."

The class grew quiet. I had goosebumps up and down my arms.

After a moment, Ms. Colman called on Hannie.

"I brought in *I Hate English*," said Hannie. "A girl named Mei Mei moves with her family from Hong Kong to New York. She feels lonely. She misses Hong Kong. English is strange to her. So she says she hates it."

"What do you think she means when she uses the word 'hate'?" asked Ms. Colman.

"I do not think she really hates English. I think she feels angry and frustrated because she cannot speak it. Since she cannot speak English, she cannot make friends. Without friends she is lonely," said Hannie.

Wheee! Wheee! Our guinea pig, Hootie, was whistling.

"I think Hootie likes that book," said Addie.

"Maybe he likes it because he is lonely

24

like Mei Mei," I said. "We do not speak guinea pig language. So Hootie has no one to talk to."

"When we go home, he stays here alone," added Natalie. "I would not like to be in an empty classroom by myself."

At the end of Hannie's book, Mei Mei learns English. Hootie could not learn English. So he could not talk with us. He would stay lonely. Poor Hootie.

6

In the Middle
of the Night

When I got home, I went straight to Grandad's room. The door was closed.

"Hi, honey," Granny whispered from behind me. "Grandad was feeling tired this afternoon. So he is taking a nap."

I tiptoed away so I would not disturb him. I wanted to tell Grandad about my day at school. But my stories would have to wait.

Grandad slept until dinnertime. Then he ate in his room. I visited with him before I went to bed.

"I am sorry I have been such a sleepy-head," said Grandad. "Come sit down and tell me how your book sharing went."

"Everyone liked my report a lot," I said. "Ms. Colman told me that *The Velveteen Rabbit* is one of her favorite stories."

"I am so glad," replied Grandad. "And what about the other books?"

I told Grandad about *My Grandson Lew*, *Everett Anderson's Goodbye*, *I Hate English*, and a few other books kids shared.

"Those sound like very good books," said Grandad. "Maybe you could borrow some from the library and read them to me."

I thought that was a gigundoly good idea. We talked some more. Then Seth told me it was my bedtime. I kissed Grandad good night.

"See you in the morning," I said.

I went upstairs and climbed into my warm, cozy little-house bed. I fell asleep right away.

A few hours later I heard the noises. I

had been sound asleep. At first I thought I was dreaming. But when I opened my eyes the noises did not stop. They were coming from downstairs. I heard people running. I heard Granny calling for help. I was confused. And scared.

"Mommy! Mommy!" I called.

"It is all right," replied Mommy. "Go back to sleep."

The next thing I heard was Granny talking on the phone. I heard the words "heart attack."

I jumped out of bed and ran to the head of the stairs. Andrew stumbled out of his room and stood next to me.

"Mommy!" I called again. "What is going on?"

"Grandad had a heart attack," replied Mommy. "You and Andrew stay upstairs."

"What did Mommy say?" asked Andrew. He was too sleepy and too little to understand. I led him back to his room and tucked him into bed.

"Everything will be all right. You go back

to sleep now," I told Andrew.

I said it just the way Mommy would say it to me. I ran to my room and took Goosie in my arms.

"Something terrible is happening to Grandad. I am so frightened," I said.

I held Goosie tightly while I listened to the voices downstairs.

Waiting Up

I could not stay in bed any longer. I got up and went back to the head of the stairs. I brought Goosie with me.

I could not hear everything the voices were saying. But I heard "still breathing" and "ambulance" and "emergency room."

"Mommy? Is Grandad going to be okay?" I called.

Mommy came to the foot of the stairs and looked up at me.

"We are taking good care of Grandad. We need you to stay upstairs. I know it is

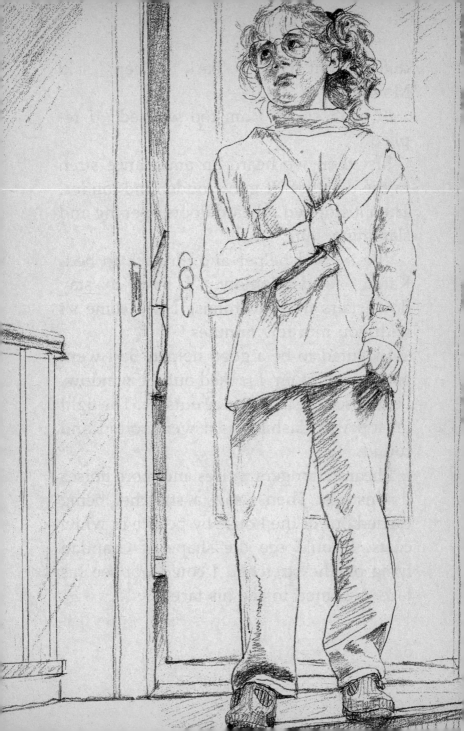

difficult, but try to go back to sleep," said Mommy.

"I can't sleep. I am too worried," I replied.

Just then we heard an ambulance siren in the distance. It grew louder and louder. Then it stopped. I heard doors opening and slamming shut.

"Be a good helper and go back to bed, Karen," said Mommy. "I have to stay downstairs now. I promise I will come sit with you in a few minutes."

I wanted to be a good helper. So I went back to my room. I looked out the window. I could see the ambulance outside. The light on top was flashing as it went round and round.

I heard strangers' voices and more noises downstairs. Then I saw a stretcher being carried out of the house by people in white coats. I could see the shape of Grandad lying on the stretcher. I could not see his face. I wanted to see his face.

They put the stretcher into the back of the ambulance. Granny climbed in. Then they closed the door and sped away. Seth followed the ambulance in his car.

"Oh, Goosie! They took Grandad away," I exclaimed.

Then I began to cry so hard I did not think I could ever stop. Mommy came in and put her arms around me. She led me to the bed and rocked me until I stopped crying.

"Will Grandad be okay?" I asked.

"I hope so," replied Mommy. "The doctors will take very good care of him at the hospital. Seth promised to call later to tell us what the doctors say."

"I want to stay up till Seth calls," I said.

"Karen, you have school tomorrow. You need your rest," replied Mommy.

"I cannot sleep, Mommy," I said. "I want to wait up with you."

Mommy took me to her room and we cuddled up in her big bed together. We rested until the phone rang. Mommy picked up the phone, said hello, then listened.

"What did Seth say? How is Grandad?" I asked when she hung up.

"Seth said Grandad is resting in the coronary intensive care unit," replied Mommy. "Seth and Granny will be coming home soon."

I knew what the coronary care unit was. Grandad had been in one before in his hospital in Nebraska. That is where they take care of anyone who has had a serious heart attack.

Suddenly I felt very tired. Mommy walked me back to my room and tucked me into bed.

"Get some rest, sweetheart," she said.

Mommy kissed me on the forehead. I fell asleep.

8

Two Good Ideas

The next day at school, I felt awfully tired. I also felt sad, worried, and confused.

Seth had called the hospital first thing in the morning. The doctors reported that Grandad's condition was very serious. They said that in the next few hours they would know more about whether he would get better.

Granny and Seth were going to spend the day at the hospital. I thought I should be there, too, in case Grandad wanted to talk to me. Mommy said she would take

Andrew and me to visit Grandad after school.

I was glad Ms. Colman picked Omar to take attendance that morning. I was too sleepy to take attendance. But I was not too sleepy to have a good idea.

"I think we should put Hootie's name in the attendance book," I said when Omar handed the book back to Ms. Colman. "After all, he is part of our class."

"I like that," said Ms. Colman. "Here, you may write his name in the book."

Cool! I was making an important addition to the class attendance book. I was finally starting to wake up and feel a little better.

"I think we should get another guinea pig to keep Hootie company," said Addie. "That way he will have someone to talk to and he will not be lonely."

Wheee! Wheee! Hootie started whistling in his cage. I think he liked Addie's idea. We all did.

"Let's talk about this," said Ms. Colman. "Are we ready to take care of two guinea pigs? It means feeding two, providing water for two, and cleaning for two."

"I am ready!" I replied.

"We will all take turns caring for the guinea pigs," said Sara.

"All right, then," said Ms. Colman. "We should try to get a male guinea pig since Hootie is a male. If we get a female, we might be overrun with baby guinea pigs."

That did not sound too bad to me. But I guessed Ms. Colman thought she would have enough babies to take care of with her own on the way.

It was Wednesday. We agreed to go to Noah's Ark pet store on Monday.

"I will call the store to make sure there are several guinea pigs for us to choose from," said Ms. Colman. "I will have permission slips for the trip ready for you tomorrow. Please make sure you give them back to me by Monday. Otherwise you will not be allowed to go to the store. Any questions?"

No one raised a hand.

"Do you have any questions, Hootie?" I asked.

Wheee! Wheee!

I do not think Hootie was asking a question. I think he was just very excited about the news.

9

Visiting Grandad

After school, Mommy was waiting outside in the car with Andrew. She was going
to drive us to the hospital.

"How is Grandad?" I asked.

"No better, no worse," Mommy replied.
"Now remember, you and Andrew will not
be allowed to go into the coronary care unit.
You will have to visit with Grandad from
the hallway."

"But I want to give him a hug and a kiss.
That always cheers him up. And maybe he
will want to hold my hand," I said.

"I am sure he would like to hold your hand, Karen," said Mommy. "But children are not allowed inside the unit. That is the rule."

Boo. I would just have to wave and blow him kisses.

Mommy parked the car in the hospital parking lot. I had been to the hospital lots of times. I was there when I broke my wrist roller skating. I was there when Nancy had her appendix out. I was there after Bobby fell through the ice on Stoneybrook pond. (That was kind of my fault because I did not warn him the ice could be thin. I was very sorry about that.)

I had been on a few different floors. But I had not been on the sixth floor yet. That was where Grandad was. And I had not been on the newborn baby floor yet. That is where Ms. Colman would be in a few months. Maybe I would get to go there then.

We stepped into the elevator and I pressed six. When we stepped out, we followed the arrows to the coronary care unit. I could see Grandad through the glass. My stomach did a flip-flop. Grandad's skin looked gray. He looked worn out. I started to cry a little and Mommy took me aside.

"Grandad will feel better if he sees you smiling," she said.

I wanted to help Grandad feel better. So I wiped away my tears and practiced smiling for Mommy.

"That is much better," she said.

Andrew and I walked to the glass wall and waved to Granny and Grandad. (Granny was sitting in a chair by the bed.) As soon as Grandad saw us, he smiled. Then he said something I could not hear. Mommy poked her head in the room to find out what he was saying. When she came back to us, she said, "Grandad wants to know how school was today."

Andrew nodded his head a lot. That was his way of saying preschool was very good.

Then it was my turn to answer. I

mouthed "Hootie." I knew Grandad would understand because we had just been talking about Hootie. I had told him how we thought Hootie was lonely.

I held up one hand to show one guinea pig. Then I held up my other hand to show a second guinea pig. Grandad understood that we were going to have two guinea pigs in my class. I was glad. I did not want him to miss out on any news while he was sick.

Then Granny came into the hall to tell us Grandad was feeling a little tired. Andrew and I waved and blew kisses to Grandad. Then we all went home.

Seth returned to the hospital after dinner, but Granny stayed home to rest. She looked as though she had grown older overnight. She looked gigundoly tired.

I went to her room to keep her company before bedtime. I sat by her side and held her hand.

"I love you and Grandad so much," I said. "I am glad you are living here. Do not worry. Grandad will be okay. Then we will all be together again."

"Grandad and I love you very much, too," replied Granny.

I kissed Granny on the cheek. Then I went upstairs to go to sleep.

10

Sad News

On Thursday morning, Mommy sat across from Andrew and me at the breakfast table.

"I have sad news to tell you," she said. "Your grandad died during the night. He simply was not strong enough to live any longer."

At first I just sat there. I was not sure I heard Mommy right. But I could tell from the look on her face that I had. I burst into tears.

"No, Mommy, no!" I said.

I cried and cried and cried. So did Andrew. Mommy held us and stroked us until we stopped.

"You do not have to go to school today if you do not want to. You can stay home with me," said Mommy. "Have your breakfast now. Then you can decide."

Andrew and I thought about it during breakfast. We both decided we would feel better if we went to school.

"I will call your teachers to tell them what has happened. That way you can talk to them if you need to," said Mommy.

When I entered my classroom Ms. Colman took me aside and said, "I am so sorry about your grandad. I am here if you need me."

After attendance Ms. Colman asked Leslie to pass out the permission slips for our trip to the pet store. Grandad would have liked to hear about our trip. I would have gone into his room after school and told him all about it. Now I would not be able to.

I started to cry a little. Leslie saw me.

"Crybaby, crybaby, dry your little eye, baby," said Leslie.

"Please go to your seat, Leslie. I will finish handing out the permission slips," said Ms. Colman.

Ms. Colman knelt beside me. She whispered in my ear, "May I tell the class about your grandad? I think it would be easier for you if they knew."

I nodded.

Ms. Colman returned to the front of the room. "I have some sad news, boys and girls," she said. "Karen's grandfather died last night. This is a very hard time for her. How many of you have lost someone close to you?"

A few kids raised their hands. I did not feel so alone with my sad news anymore.

"How did you feel then?" asked Ms. Colman.

The kids took turns telling how they had felt. Sad. Lonely. Frightened.

"My dog, Rusty, got run over by a car,"

said Ian. "At first I did not feel anything at all. Then I started crying so hard."

"We are talking about difficult feelings," said Ms. Colman. "Sometimes we do not want to face them. It is better if we do. It helps to share them, too."

"Right after my grandma Betsy died, I felt sad all the time," said Audrey. "Then after a while, I started to feel better. I think about Grandma Betsy a lot. So she is sort of still with me."

"So you know some of the feelings Karen might be having now," said Ms. Colman. "Maybe you will try to help her to feel better."

Natalie touched my arm and smiled at me. Then Ricky passed me a note. It was from Leslie. It said, "I am sorry." I turned to her and smiled. My classmates were being gigundoly nice.

"I am going to read the book that Ricky brought to class on Monday," said Ms. Colman. "It is called *Everett Anderson's Goodbye*."

I liked listening to the story. I especially liked hearing the end again: *"Whatever happens when people die, love doesn't stop, and neither will I."*

After school I went home and cried and slept and slept and cried. And then I started to feel a little bit better.

Saying Good-bye

Saturday was Grandad's funeral.

"Are you sure you want to go?" asked Seth when I finished eating breakfast. "You do not have to go, you know. It is perfectly all right for you to stay home."

Mommy and Seth had told me the night before what the funeral would be like. They said that Grandad would be in a casket. A minister would say a few words about Grandad, and then some prayers. Then everyone would drive to the cemetery. The minister would say more prayers and we would put flowers on the casket. This sounded like a very good way to say good-bye.

"I want to be there," I said.

Andrew had decided to stay home. Kristy was going to baby-sit for him.

I went upstairs to get dressed. I put on my navy blue jumper and tights, a white turtleneck shirt, and my shiny black dress-up shoes.

Mommy peeked into my room to see if I needed any help. I did not. I was ready to go.

"You look so pretty, Karen," said Mommy. "I know Grandad would be proud of you."

I cried a little because Grandad could not see me.

A few minutes later, Daddy brought Kristy to the little house. He gave Andrew and me big hugs. Then he gave Mommy, Seth, and Granny beautiful flowers and told them how sorry he was that Grandad had died.

The rest of the day went by in a blur.

We drove to the funeral parlor in Stoney-brook. Mommy's and Seth's friends came to the service. Some of them brought flowers. (Granny's and Grandad's friends were in Nebraska.)

The minister said kind words and a few prayers just the way Mommy and Seth had said he would. He even said my name. He called Andrew and me Grandad's beloved grandchildren. That made me feel proud.

The next thing I knew we were in the car again, driving from the funeral parlor to the cemetery. It was windy and cold at the cemetary. But it was pretty and quiet, too. The minister handed us each a flower. He said more prayers. We took turns putting our flowers on the casket. By the time we were done, it looked very beautiful.

I felt bad for Granny. I could see she was trying to be brave. But she looked sad and lost. Seth put his arm around her. I slipped my hand into hers. Mommy put her arm

around me. We huddled together in the cold.

"It is time to go now," said Mommy.

I waved good-bye to my grandad. Then we turned and started home.

12

A Friend for Hootie

When I woke up on Monday I did not feel so good. Mommy felt my forehead.

"Honey, you do not have a fever. You are probably worn out from the weekend," she said. "You can go to school if you like and rest when you come home."

I definitely wanted to go to school. It was the day of our trip to the pet store. We were going to get a friend for Hootie.

I dressed, ate a little breakfast, and met Nancy at the bus stop. I felt better by the time we reached school.

Omar's father was in the room talking to Ms. Colman. Mr. Harris had taken the morning off from work to come with us on our trip. He had come with us to the pet store when we picked out Hootie, too.

"All right, class, please settle down," said Ms. Colman. "I am going to assign partners. The bus will be here any minute."

I got to be partners with Hannie. Nancy was partners with Audrey. We were going to sit in one whole row across the bus.

"Please remember our bus rules," said Ms. Colman. "Stay in your seats. No hands out windows. And no shouting. The bus driver needs to concentrate."

We marched out of the classroom and onto the yellow bus that was waiting outside. As soon as we were on our way, we started singing one of our favorite bus songs, "A Hundred Bottles of Pop on the Wall." We were down to thirty-six bottles of pop by the time we reached the pet store.

Mr. Hanley, the store manager, was waiting outside. (We had met him before when we came to buy Hootie.)

"Welcome," he said. "I have some excellent guinea pigs to choose from today."

Get ready, guinea pigs! One of you will soon have a new home and a new friend named Hootie.

As soon as we reached the guinea pig cages, we knew we had a problem. The guinea pigs were *all* cute. They were whistling and playing. One was drinking from the water bottle. Another was gnawing on a piece of wood. (Guinea pigs' front teeth just keep growing and growing. That is why they need safe things to gnaw on. Gnawing wears down their teeth.)

"I like that black one," said Ricky.

"But look at the brown one. He is so cute," said Addie.

"The white one is looking right at us," said Natalie. "He wants to come home with us."

"We can only buy one," said Ms. Colman. "We will take a vote."

Ms. Colman pointed to each guinea pig. Mr. Harris counted up the votes. A nice fat black, white, and brown guinea pig won. Hooray! He was the one I voted for.

"You picked one of my favorites," said Mr. Hanley. "He arrived here just two days ago and is quite friendly."

We used money from our class fund to buy a food cup, water bottle, and toys for our new guinea pig. We already had everything else we needed.

When we returned to school, we thanked Mr. Harris for coming with us. (He had to get back to his office.) Then we put our new pet into the cage with Hootie.

Sniff, sniff, went the new guinea pig.

Wheee! Wheee! went Hootie.

Sniff, sniff! Wheee! Wheee!

"I think they like each other already," said Hannie.

There was one thing left to do. We had to name our new guinea pig. I had an idea.

"How about Everett after Everett Anderson?" I said.

Ms. Colman smiled. "All in favor, say, 'Everett'!" she said.

"Everett!" the class cried.

Welcome to second grade, Everett Guinea Pig.

13

A Surprising Announcement

By Wednesday, Hootie and Everett seemed like old friends. Now that Hootie had company, he was acting more cheerful.

I was glad for Hootie. But watching him cheer up with his new companion made me think about Granny. I knew she was lonely without *her* companion. I felt sad for her.

Everett seemed as happy as Hootie. We did notice that he had grown fatter since we got him. He had been fat to begin with. That is probably why he moved so slowly.

But he had an amazing appetite, so he was probably healthy.

I could tell Ms. Colman was worried about Everett, though. I saw a pile of guinea pig books on her desk. When we returned from recess that day, Mrs. Chen, the sixth-grade science teacher, was kneeling by the guinea pig cage examining Everett.

I rushed into the room.

"Is Everett okay?" I asked.

"I am sure he is fine," replied Ms. Colman. "I just wanted to ask Mrs. Chen about his weight. Everyone, please sit down. I need a moment to speak with Mrs. Chen."

Mrs. Chen picked up Everett and turned him over. Then she petted him. She and Ms. Colman were whispering to each other. Then they smiled. That was a good sign. It meant that nothing too serious could be wrong with our new guinea pig.

"Thank you for coming, Mrs. Chen," said Ms. Colman. She walked Mrs. Chen to the door, then turned to us.

"Class, I have an announcement to make," said Ms. Colman.

From the look on Ms. Colman's face, I could tell this was going to be one of her excellent Surprising Announcements. Goody.

"I have a report for you about Everett. It turns out that Everett is not a boy guinea pig. Everett is a girl. And she is going to have babies," said Ms. Colman.

"Wow! When will the babies be born?" I asked.

"Very soon," Ms. Colman replied. "Mrs. Chen thinks they could be here as early as next week."

"Do we have to give her extra vitamins, or anything?" asked Natalie.

"That is very thoughtful," replied Ms. Colman. "Her regular diet is just fine. But we do need to put her in a cage of her own. Mrs. Chen has an extra cage we can borrow. One of the sixth-grade students will drop it off later."

"Are we still going to call her Everett?"

asked Nancy. "That is a boy's name."

We all agreed that Everett was no longer a good name for our guinea pig. She needed a girl's name. We wanted to give her a name that sounded like Everett, though. We thought of Evelyn, Eve, and Evita. We took a vote. Evelyn won.

Hmm. Now Ms. Colman was not the only one expecting a baby. Evelyn was pregnant, too. I thought about suggesting a baby shower for our guinea pig. But I knew there was not enough time for that. Mrs. Chen said the babies would be here any day. I could hardly wait.

14

Babies!

I was the first one to arrive at our room on Thursday. I raced to Evelyn's cage. No babies. I kept my eye on Evelyn all day. Nothing happened.

I was the first one to arrive at our room on Friday. I raced to Evelyn's cage.

"She did it! Evelyn had her babies!" I shouted.

"Shh. You will scare them," said Natalie when she arrived.

Everyone crowded around. Then Ms. Colman came into the room. We all looked

at Evelyn's babies. There were six. Two were white. One was black. Two were brown and white, like Hootie. One was all three colors, like Evelyn. They did not look as babyish as some other baby animals I had seen.

A cat once moved into the toolshed at the big house to have its kittens. At first, the kittens did not look so cute to me. They were scraggly. Their eyes were closed. They did not look cute and fluffy for several weeks.

But these guinea pigs looked perfectly fine. Their eyes were open. They were walking around. They were just very small.

Evelyn was nursing three of them. She was licking another one's coat.

"They are so-o-o cute," said Hannie.

"Can I hold one?" asked Bobby.

"I do not think that would be a good idea," said Ms. Colman. "I know this is very exciting. But right now I would like you all to sit down. Evelyn and her babies need to rest. We can talk about the babies a little bit. Then we must get to work."

Ms. Colman picked up one of her guinea pig books and read to us from it.

"Guinea pigs in the wild usually have one to four young," she read. "But when they are in captivity — which means when they are in cages — they can have up to eight young. The babies each weigh about three ounces. The mother takes care of them for about three weeks."

"Our mothers care for us a lot longer than that," said Addie.

"Thank goodness. I would hate to have to cook my own dinner," said Hank.

Everybody laughed.

"Can we keep the babies?" asked Pamela.

"I am afraid not," replied Ms. Colman. "Two guinea pigs are enough for one classroom. When the babies are ready, they must go to new homes."

"Whose homes will they go to?" I asked.

"I have not decided that yet," said Ms. Colman. "I will think about it and let you know soon."

15

Talking to Granny

On Friday night, I dreamed I was telling Grandad about the guinea pigs. When I woke up on Saturday morning, I started to go downstairs to tell him some more.

Then I remembered he was gone. A whole week had passed since his funeral.

I looked for Granny so I could say good morning to her. I looked in the kitchen. She was usually one of the first people up. Mommy and Seth were drinking their coffee. But they were alone.

"Where is Granny?" I asked.

"She is in her room," replied Seth. "I am sure she would be happy to see you."

I knocked on Granny's door and poked my head in. She looked so sad and lonely. I wondered how long Granny would feel that way.

"Do you want some company?" I asked.

"Sure," Granny replied.

I climbed into the bed and snuggled up beside her. I told her my dream.

"Grandad would have loved hearing about those guinea pigs," said Granny.

Granny told me she had a dream about Grandad, too. She dreamed he was working in his garden. All of a sudden tomatoes popped up all over the place.

"He would have liked that! He would have made lots of tomato sauce and put it in jars," I said.

Grandad liked to cook.

We talked some more about the things Grandad liked best. Granny said that spending time with Andrew and me was at the top of his list.

After a while Granny and I joined Mommy, Seth, and Andrew in the kitchen.

My family spent the day together. We talked and read. We bundled up in warm clothes and took a walk around the neighborhood. We ate lunch. Granny took a nap in the afternoon. Then, for a treat, Seth took us out to dinner. We went to Uncle Ed's Chinese Restaurant downtown.

We ordered a few dishes to share. Andrew and I ate crunchy noodles in sweet sauce while the grown-ups talked.

"Have you thought about the things you might like to do now?" Mommy asked Granny. "Maybe you could try some volunteer work. The library always needs people to help out."

"Yes, that sounds nice," replied Granny.

I am not even sure Granny had heard what Mommy said.

"We could make your downstairs room into a permanent bedroom," said Seth. "We would fix it up just the way you like it. You are welcome to stay as long as you want."

"Thank you," replied Granny. "But I am used to living in a house of my own. I will need a bit more independence than that."

"There are other choices," said Mommy. "I think you are too independent to move into Stoneybrook Manor. But there are apartment complexes here where many people your age live. If you moved to one of them, you could make new friends more easily."

Granny did not belong at Stoneybrook Manor. I had visited the manor with my class. It was very nice, but the people there are not able to live on their own. Granny is not like that.

Nannie had lived in one of the apartment complexes for a little while. I had liked it. It was not too far away. I hoped Granny would choose a place like that to move to.

"There are so many choices," said Granny. "I will just have to think everything over."

The waiter brought our food. It was very delicious. When we finished eating, he brought a plate of sliced oranges and fortune cookies.

I opened my cookie and read my fortune out loud. It said, "Exciting days lie ahead." Goody.

"Now read your fortune, Granny," I said.

Granny's fortune said, "The answers will come."

"I hope so," said Granny. "Right now, all I have are the questions."

16

The Lottery

I ran into our classroom on Monday to see how Evelyn and her babies were doing. They were fine.

After attendance, Ms. Colman said, "I have thought of a way to find homes for the guinea pigs. We will hold a lottery for both of the second-grade classes. Whoever gets permission from their parents can take part."

All right! A lottery sounded like fun.

"Why does Mr. Berger's class get to be in the lottery?" asked Pamela.

"Because I do not think six students from our class alone will get permission to take home a pet," said Ms. Colman.

Hmm. A gigundoly good idea was coming to me. I wondered if I could bring home a guinea pig if I did not plan to keep it myself. I did not think that would be a problem. Especially if I had permission from Mommy and Seth.

The person I wanted to win a guinea pig for was Granny. A pet is very good company when a person is lonely. Granny could take her guinea pig with her wherever she decided to live.

When I got home from school that day I waited until Mommy and Seth and I were alone. Then I told them my idea.

"That is very thoughtful of you," said Seth. "A pet for Granny sounds like a nice idea."

"I usually do not approve of giving pets as surprise gifts," said Mommy. "A pet is a responsibility. The person who is getting the pet needs to agree to take that responsibility on."

"But a guinea pig is not too hard to take care of. It is not like having a dog you have to walk," I said.

"You are right," said Seth. "And it is such a good idea, I think it is worth taking a chance on," said Seth.

Mommy agreed and signed the permission slip for me.

"Hooray! Now all I have to do is win," I said.

The lottery was held on Thursday. Three other kids from my class got permission to take a guinea pig home. They were Sara, Omar, and Audrey. Five kids in Mr. Berger's class got permission.

Ms. Colman collected the permission slips and dropped them into a big jar. Mr. Berger and his class came to our room for the drawing. (They had been invited in to meet the guinea pigs on Tuesday.)

"We are ready to begin," said Ms. Colman. She picked a name from the jar.

"Congratulations, Liddie Yuan. You are our first winner." (Liddie is in Mr. Berger's class.)

Everyone clapped for Liddie. Mr. Berger picked the next name.

"Our second winner is Omar Harris. Congratulations, Omar," said Mr. Berger.

We clapped again. Two down, four to go. I was getting nervous. I wanted to win a guinea pig for Granny so badly.

It was Ms. Colman's turn to pick a name.

"Congratulations, Karen Brewer," said Ms. Colman.

"Yippee!!" I shouted.

Audrey won the fourth guinea pig. Then two more kids from Mr. Berger's class won.

Sara was the only kid from our class who did not win a guinea pig. She looked very disappointed. I felt bad for her. But I was glad I had won the guinea pig for Granny. She needed a soft guinea pig who wiggled its nose to cheer her up.

17

Granny's News

Clink, clink! It was dinnertime at the little house. I was about to make my Surprising Announcement. I tapped my glass to get everyone's attention.

"Granny, do you remember when I told you that Evelyn had six guinea pigs?" I said.

"Yes," replied Granny. "I remember."

"Well, you are now the proud owner of one," I said.

I waited for Granny's face to light up. It did not. In fact, it kind of drooped.

"That was very thoughtful of you,

Karen," said Granny. "But I have some important news to share. This seems like a good time to share it."

"What is it?" asked Seth.

"I have decided what I want to do. I am going to return to the farm in Nebraska," said Granny.

Mommy and Seth looked completely surprised.

"All by yourself?" asked Seth.

Granny nodded.

"Why go there alone when you have us here?" asked Mommy. "We are your family. We love you."

"I appreciate that," said Granny. "Really I do. But Grandad and I lived in Nebraska for a long time. I have many years of memories there."

"How will you run the farm on your own?" asked Seth.

"The farm is run by hired hands now. So there are always people around," replied Granny. "I miss my gardens and my animals. It is where I belong."

Mommy, Seth, and Granny talked some more about what Granny's life would be like if she lived on the farm or stayed here in Stoneybrook. In the end, they all agreed that Granny would be happier back in Nebraska.

I felt sad that Granny would be leaving. But I wanted her to be where she would be happy.

"You can still have the guinea pig, Granny," I said. "A guinea pig would love to live on a farm."

Granny took my hand.

"It is so sweet of you to have won a guinea pig for me," said Granny. "But I do not want to fly him all the way back to Nebraska when I have so many animals there waiting for me."

Granny was right. She did not really need the guinea pig if she was going back to the farm.

I had a pet rat and a goldfish. So I did not need him either. Hmm. I had a brand-new gigundoly good idea.

18

Karen's Gift

On Tuesday morning, Mommy said, "Have you decided what to do about the guinea pig?"

"I have a very good plan," I replied.

I could hardly wait to get to school. I ate my breakfast fast. (That did not get me to school any earlier. The bus still came at the same time.)

I rode the bus with Nancy. As soon as we reached school, I called, "Meet you inside!"

I raced into the room. (That did not do

any good either. The person I wanted to see was not there yet.)

I waited. And waited. The person I wanted to see arrived later than usual. I caught her on the way to her seat.

"Hi, Sara! I have something to tell you," I blurted out. "The guinea pig I won was not going to be for me. I wanted him to be a gift for my grandma. But my grandma cannot take him. So I want him to be a gift for someone else. Guess who!"

"Who?" asked Sara.

"You!" I replied. "I know you really wanted to have a guinea pig. And now you can."

"I cannot believe it," said Sara. "That is so nice of you. Thank you, Karen."

"You are welcome," I replied. "I know you will take very good care of him."

"Oh, I will. You can come over to visit him any time," said Sara. She had a big smile on her face.

Just then, Ms. Colman said, "Would you like to take attendance today, Karen?"

"Sure!" I replied. "And I will add Evelyn's name to our book."

I finished in no time. (I am very good at taking attendance.)

"I would like to continue our unit on feelings this morning," said Ms. Colman. "Let's start with you, Sara. You have a big smile on your face. Will you tell the class why?"

Sara told everyone about the guinea pig gift.

"I was really disappointed when I did not win a guinea pig yesterday. But I am so happy today. I think getting the guinea pig from Karen is even better than winning one," said Sara.

"We can learn something about feelings from this," said Ms. Colman. "Feelings can change from one day to the next. They can even change from one minute to the next."

I raised my hand. Ms. Colman called on me.

"That is good to know in case you are feeling bad," I said. "You might feel happy a few minutes later."

"Good point," said Ms. Colman. "We can also see how one person can affect another person's feelings. For example, one person can hurt another person or make him feel angry. Or one person can make another person feel good, the way Karen made Sara feel today."

"Or the way Evelyn makes Hootie feel happy," said Addie.

"Exactly," replied Ms. Colman. "I would like you to do some homework tonight. I would like you to keep track of your feelings from the time you leave school today until the time you get home. I think you will be surprised at how many feelings you have even in that short time."

Just then, Natalie kicked me under the desk. For a minute I felt annoyed. Then Natalie apologized. I felt better.

I turned to wave to Hannie and Nancy.

They waved back. I felt good. Sara waved, too. I felt terrific.

Ms. Colman announced a surprise math quiz. Ooh. I felt nervous.

Oh, boy. I was having feelings all over the place!

19

The Airport

It was a Saturday at the end of February. It had been a week and a half since Granny had told us her plan to move back to Nebraska. Now she was all packed and ready to go.

"I will miss you so much," I said. "I will call you a lot, okay?"

"I am counting on it," Granny replied.

Seth was loading Granny's bags into his car. We were going to drive to the airport to see Granny off.

I remembered when she and Grandad

had arrived before Thanksgiving. Grandad was so tired, he needed a wheelchair to get around the airport even then. Now Granny was going home alone. It was so sad.

"Here, Granny. I made this for you," I said.

I handed Granny a homemade guinea pig. I had drawn a baby guinea pig on a piece of paper. I glued cotton on it, so it would feel very soft when Granny petted it.

"He is very easy to care for," I said, smiling. "The only thing he needs is a name."

"I know what I would like to name the guinea pig. Are you sure it's a boy?" asked Granny.

"Well, she is looking a little fat today," I replied. "Maybe she is a girl after all."

"Good. Then I can name her Karen Junior," said Granny.

"I think that is a very good name!" I replied.

Seth stuck his head into the room.

Mommy and Andrew were standing behind him with their coats on.

"Is everyone ready to go?" asked Seth.

Granny took one last look around the room.

"This was a very nice place to live," she said. "There was a lot of love in this room. I will miss it."

"It will always be here for you," said Seth.

"If you get lonesome, just get on a plane. We will meet you at the airport," said Mommy.

"I'm hot," said Andrew.

Granny laughed.

"You are all bundled up. Let's go," she said.

On the way to the airport, Granny told us about the things she was looking forward to returning to.

"I will be happy to hear the rooster crowing in the morning," said Granny.

"Pearl the cat will be happy you are

home," said Andrew. (Andrew likes Pearl the cat.)

"Tell Tia I will write to her soon," I said. (Tia is the friend I made when I visited Nebraska.)

"Please give our best to the chickens and the cows," said Seth, smiling.

"What will you tell the animals when they ask for Grandad?" asked Andrew.

"I believe animals know about things like dying," replied Granny. "I will tell them the truth and they will understand."

We started noticing planes flying low. Then we saw arrows pointing to the airport. Before we knew it, we were walking Granny to her gate.

I tried to be brave and not cry. But I could not help it. I just felt too sad seeing Granny leave.

We were all crying — Granny, Mommy, Seth, Andrew, and I. We gave each other a five-way hug.

"Flight two-oh-one to Omaha now boarding," said a voice over the loudspeaker.

90

Seth took Granny's hand and walked her to the gate. Granny turned to wave.

"Wait! I have one more thing to give you," I said.

I ran to Granny and put a copy of *Everett Anderson's Goodbye* in her hand.

"Read it when you are missing Grandad," I said. "I think it will make you feel better."

"Thank you," said Granny.

Then she turned and slowly walked to the plane.

20

New Homes

By Wednesday morning, I had already spoken to Granny three times on the phone. She was doing her best trying to get used to her new-old life.

"How are you feeling today?" I had asked the last time we spoke. "Did you see Tia yet?"

"Yes," replied Granny. "Tia's family invited me over for lunch yesterday. It was a very nice visit. Tia asks you to write soon."

I promised to call Granny again when I got home from school. On Wednesday

93

afternoon the baby guinea pigs were going to their new homes. Granny wanted to hear about it.

When I arrived at school I was so excited about the guinea pigs, it was hard for me to keep still. I kept turning around and waving to Sara. I used every excuse I could think of to get up from my desk. Then I would peek at Evelyn's babies.

By the end of the day, Ms. Colman had reminded me three times to use my indoor voice and twice had asked me to return to my seat. (She asked nicely every time. That is why Ms. Colman is a gigundoly wonderful teacher.)

"All right, class," she said. "It is time to get the guinea pigs ready to go to their new homes. Karen, would you please go to Mr. Berger's class and invite in the children who won guinea pigs?"

The six new owners walked to Evelyn's cage. (The rest of us stood back and watched.) They were each asked to point to the guinea pig they wanted. If two kids wanted the same guinea pig, they would have to draw straws to see who got it.

Sara picked a round little guinea pig with the same markings Evelyn had. Liddie Yuan wanted that one, too, so they had to draw straws. Sara won.

Sara's father arrived carrying a brand-new cage with fresh wood shavings.

"Hi, Daddy," said Sara. "Come see my guinea pig."

"He is very good-looking," said Mr. Ford.

Ms. Colman gently lifted out the guinea pig and put it into the cage. Sara covered the cage with a heavy towel, so the baby would not get cold.

"Thanks again, Karen. Don't forget to visit us soon," said Sara.

"I won't," I replied.

Five more guinea pigs were gently lifted out and put into special carriers. When they were all gone, Ms. Colman set Evelyn's cage on the floor next to Hootie's. That way the guinea pigs could look at each other.

"Wheee! Wheee!" said Hootie.

"Wheee! Wheee!" said Evelyn.

Hootie and Evelyn seemed happy. I knew Sara was *very* happy.

I thought about Granny. Most days she felt sad. But maybe, like Everett Anderson, she would feel better in time. I hoped some day I would see her happy again. Because that would make me happy, too.

About the Author

ANN M. MARTIN lives in New York City and loves animals, especially cats. She has a cat of her own, Gussie.

Other books by Ann M. Martin that you might enjoy are *Stage Fright*; *Me and Katie (the Pest)*; and the books in *The Baby-sitters Club* series.

Ann likes ice cream and *I Love Lucy*. And she has her own little sister, whose name is Jane.

Little Sister

Don't miss #71

KAREN'S ISLAND ADVENTURE

The first thing I noticed when we stepped off the plane was the temperature. It was *hot*. And the sun. It was *bright*.

I dug into my knapsack and pulled out my new sunglasses. They had yellow frames with white speckles. When I put them on I felt like a glamorous movie star on a tropical vacation. I held my arms out wide and lifted my chin in the air.

"Halloo, dahlings," I said. "Which way to Palm Isle?"

Beep! Beep! A van with "Palm Isle Resort" written on the side was waiting at the curb. The van was turquoise with brightly colored fruits painted on the side.

The driver had very dark skin and a big friendly smile. He welcomed his passengers to St. Philip.

LITTLE APPLE®

BABY-SITTERS
Little Sister™
by Ann M. Martin, author of *The Baby-sitters Club*®

☐	MQ44300-3	#1	Karen's Witch	$2.95
☐	MQ44259-7	#2	Karen's Roller Skates	$2.95
☐	MQ44299-7	#3	Karen's Worst Day	$2.95
☐	MQ44264-3	#4	Karen's Kittycat Club	$2.95
☐	MQ44258-9	#5	Karen's School Picture	$2.95
☐	MQ44298-8	#6	Karen's Little Sister	$2.95
☐	MQ44257-0	#7	Karen's Birthday	$2.95
☐	MQ42670-2	#8	Karen's Haircut	$2.95
☐	MQ43652-X	#9	Karen's Sleepover	$2.95
☐	MQ43651-1	#10	Karen's Grandmothers	$2.95
☐	MQ43650-3	#11	Karen's Prize	$2.95
☐	MQ43649-X	#12	Karen's Ghost	$2.95
☐	MQ43648-1	#13	Karen's Surprise	$2.95
☐	MQ43646-5	#14	Karen's New Year	$2.95
☐	MQ43645-7	#15	Karen's in Love	$2.95
☐	MQ43644-9	#16	Karen's Goldfish	$2.95
☐	MQ43643-0	#17	Karen's Brothers	$2.95
☐	MQ43642-2	#18	Karen's Home Run	$2.95
☐	MQ43641-4	#19	Karen's Good-Bye	$2.95
☐	MQ44823-4	#20	Karen's Carnival	$2.95
☐	MQ44824-2	#21	Karen's New Teacher	$2.95
☐	MQ44833-1	#22	Karen's Little Witch	$2.95
☐	MQ44832-3	#23	Karen's Doll	$2.95
☐	MQ44859-5	#24	Karen's School Trip	$2.95
☐	MQ44831-5	#25	Karen's Pen Pal	$2.95
☐	MQ44830-7	#26	Karen's Ducklings	$2.75
☐	MQ44829-3	#27	Karen's Big Joke	$2.95
☐	MQ44828-5	#28	Karen's Tea Party	$2.95
☐	MQ44825-0	#29	Karen's Cartwheel	$2.75
☐	MQ45645-8	#30	Karen's Kittens	$2.95
☐	MQ45646-6	#31	Karen's Bully	$2.95
☐	MQ45647-4	#32	Karen's Pumpkin Patch	$2.95
☐	MQ45648-2	#33	Karen's Secret	$2.95
☐	MQ45650-4	#34	Karen's Snow Day	$2.95
☐	MQ45652-0	#35	Karen's Doll Hospital	$2.95
☐	MQ45651-2	#36	Karen's New Friend	$2.95
☐	MQ45653-9	#37	Karen's Tuba	$2.95
☐	MQ45655-5	#38	Karen's Big Lie	$2.95
☐	MQ45654-7	#39	Karen's Wedding	$2.95
☐	MQ47040-X	#40	Karen's Newspaper	$2.95

More Titles...

The Baby-sitters Little Sister titles continued...

❑ MQ47041-8	#41	Karen's School	$2.95
❑ MQ47042-6	#42	Karen's Pizza Party	$2.95
❑ MQ46912-6	#43	Karen's Toothache	$2.95
❑ MQ47043-4	#44	Karen's Big Weekend	$2.95
❑ MQ47044-2	#45	Karen's Twin	$2.95
❑ MQ47045-0	#46	Karen's Baby-sitter	$2.95
❑ MQ46913-4	#47	Karen's Kite	$2.95
❑ MQ47046-9	#48	Karen's Two Families	$2.95
❑ MQ47047-7	#49	Karen's Stepmother	$2.95
❑ MQ47048-5	#50	Karen's Lucky Penny	$2.95
❑ MQ48229-7	#51	Karen's Big Top	$2.95
❑ MQ48299-8	#52	Karen's Mermaid	$2.95
❑ MQ48300-5	#53	Karen's School Bus	$2.95
❑ MQ48301-3	#54	Karen's Candy	$2.95
❑ MQ48230-0	#55	Karen's Magician	$2.95
❑ MQ48302-1	#56	Karen's Ice Skates	$2.95
❑ MQ48303-X	#57	Karen's School Mystery	$2.95
❑ MQ48304-8	#58	Karen's Ski Trip	$2.95
❑ MQ48231-9	#59	Karen's Leprechaun	$2.95
❑ MQ48305-6	#60	Karen's Pony	$2.95
❑ MQ48306-4	#61	Karen's Tattletale	$2.95
❑ MQ48307-2	#62	Karen's New Bike	$2.95
❑ MQ25996-2	#63	Karen's Movie	$2.95
❑ MQ25997-0	#64	Karen's Lemonade Stand	$2.95
❑ MQ25998-9	#65	Karen's Toys	$2.95
❑ MQ26279-3	#66	Karen's Monsters	$2.95
❑ MQ43647-3		Karen's Wish Super Special #1	$3.25
❑ MQ44834-X		Karen's Plane Trip Super Special #2	$3.25
❑ MQ44827-7		Karen's Mystery Super Special #3	$3.25
❑ MQ45644-X		Karen's Three Musketeers Super Special #4	$2.95
❑ MQ45649-0		Karen's Baby Super Special #5	$3.25
❑ MQ46911-8		Karen's Campout Super Special #6	$3.25